Safari Animals™

LIONS

Amelie von Zumbusch

PowerKiDS press

New York

Published in 2007 by The Rosen Publishing Group, Inc.
29 East 21st Street, New York, NY 10010

First Edition

Book Design: Erica Clendening

Photo Credits: Cover, pp. 1, 5, 9, 11, 13, 15, 21, 24 (top left, top right, bottom right) © Digital Vision; p. 7, 24 (bottom left) © Digital Stock; pp. 17, 19, 23 © Artville.

Library of Congress Cataloging-in-Publication Data

Zumbusch, Amelie von.
  Lions / Amelie von Zumbusch. — 1st ed.
      p. cm. — (Safari animals)
  Includes index.
  ISBN-13: 978-1-4042-3612-7 (library binding)
  ISBN-10: 1-4042-3612-0 (library binding)
  1. Lions—Juvenile literature. I. Title.

  QL737.C23Z79547 2007
  599.757—dc22

                                        2006020175

Manufactured in the United States of America

Contents

Lions are members of the cat family. They are big and strong.

Lions live in Africa. Most lions live on the grassy savannah.

Male lions have a mane of hair around their face.

A group of lions is called a pride. The members of a pride work together.

Mother lions have from two to four babies at a time. Baby lions are called cubs.

Lion cubs like to chase each other. They also like to climb trees.

Lions eat meat. They track other animals for food.

Lions have big teeth. They use these teeth to catch their food.

Lions need water as well as food. They lap water up with their tongues.

Lions spend much of the day napping. Sometimes they sleep in trees.

Words to Know

mane

pride

savannah

tongue

Web Sites

Due to the changing nature of Internet links, PowerKids Press has developed an online list of Web sites related to this book. This site is updated regularly. Please use this link to access the list: www.powerkidslinks.com/safari/lion/